First Hardcover Edition, June 2016

ISBN 978-1-4847-1554-3
FAC-038091-16123
Library of Congress Control Number: 2015952434
Printed in the USA
For more Disney Press fun, visit www.disneybooks.com

SUSTAINABLE FORESTRY INITIATIVE   Certified Sourcing
www.sfiprogram.org
SFI-00993
This Label Applies to Text Stock Only

Disney

ELENA
~ and the ~
Secret of Avalor

Written by Craig Gerber & Catherine Hapka

Illustrated by Grace Lee

Disney PRESS

Los Angeles • New York

I'm Sofia.

I discovered a secret library filled with real-life stories that needed happy endings. Now I'm the Storykeeper, and I'm in charge of making those endings happen.

One day the library shows me a book called
The Lost Princess of Avalor.

"Like my Amulet of Avalor?" I wonder.

Suddenly, a wizard appears!

"Exactly like your amulet," he says.
"I am Alacazar. I was once the
Royal Wizard of the kingdom of Avalor."

Alacazar tells me his story.

"Forty-one years ago, in the kingdom of Avalor, there
lived a princess named Elena," he begins. "One day,
her kingdom was invaded by an **evil sorceress** named
Shuriki. Elena bravely challenged Shuriki, which gave me
time to protect her sister, Isabel, and their grandparents.

"The Amulet of Avalor protected the princess from Shuriki by pulling Elena inside it."

"So Princess Elena is **trapped** inside my amulet?" I ask.

"Yes," Alacazar replies. "And you are the special princess who was chosen to free her."

I have to help Princess Elena! So I hurry to find my family. Somehow I have to convince them to travel to Avalor!

When Mom and Dad say yes, I'm so excited, but I'm nervous, too. I hope I'll be able to free Elena once we make it to Avalor.

Avalor City is the most amazing kingdom I've ever seen! Alacazar told me to find his old house and then summon his spirit guide. But how will I find the wizard's house in such a huge city? And **what** is a spirit guide?

When we arrive at the dock, Queen Shuriki and Chancellor Esteban are there to greet us. Shuriki smiles and the crowd cheers, but the people don't look very happy. "It is an honor that you have chosen to visit my humble kingdom," Shuriki says. Then she invites us to the palace.

We're having lunch on the terrace when some strange creatures fly overhead. "They are jaquins," a servant explains. "Magical creatures that are the symbols of Avalor."

Suddenly, the jaquins swoop down and grab food off the table.

Shuriki is furious. "Get out of here, you **pests!**"

When the others go inside the palace, I stay back.
"Excuse me," I call to the jaquins. "Can you help me?"
"We don't help friends of Shuriki," one of them says. But
when I tell them I came here to rescue Princess Elena, the
jaquins are surprised! They thought Elena was gone forever.

"We'll do anything to help Princess Elena," declares a jaquin named Skylar. So I ask them to take me to Alacazar's house.

When we get there, I meet Mateo, Alacazar's grandson. He offers to help rescue Elena, too!

Mateo has been practicing to become a wizard and summons a spirit animal named Zuzo. So that's what Alacazar meant! Zuzo tells me I have to steal Shuriki's wand. Then I need to find the statue of Aziluna in an ancient temple. And when I place the wand and my amulet on the statue, Elena will be set free.

Back at the palace, I convince Shuriki to **dance** with me.

Then I take her **wand!**

With the wand held tight, I head to the temple.
Inside is an enchanted lake. The statue
must be in the water!

"Being a mermaid sure
would come in handy right now."
I touch my amulet.

Magically, I turn into one! As I start swimming,
the statue begins to rise up out of the water!
I wrap my amulet around the wand, place it
on the statue, and then . . .

Princess Elena appears!

"I knew you would free me, Sofia," she cries.

"Thank you!"

"You're welcome!" I say, putting my amulet back on.

It's pink now. Elena takes Shuriki's wand.

"Now it's up to me to free my kingdom!"

We fly to the palace, but my jaquin can't keep up. So Elena will have to face Shuriki alone.

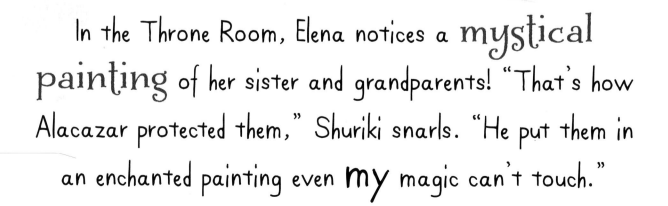

In the Throne Room, Elena notices a mystical painting of her sister and grandparents! "That's how Alacazar protected them," Shuriki snarls. "He put them in an enchanted painting even my magic can't touch."

Shuriki grabs back her wand and then tells the guards to seize Elena. But Skylar bursts in and flies Elena out of the palace. "I want her captured by nightfall!" Shuriki shouts. "Her and that little princess, Sofia."

My parents protest, but Shuriki tells her guards to lock them up.

My jaquin and I catch up to Elena and Skylar, and we go back to Mateo's house. When I ask Elena what happened, she shakes her head sadly. "I tried my best," she says, "but Shuriki has your family. I'm so sorry."

She has my family? Oh, no!

Just then, Mateo's mother arrives with friends who heard about Princess Elena's return.

As I look around, I can see that
Elena's friends would do **anything** for her.
"We can all face Shuriki together!" I say.

So Elena comes up with a plan. . . .

For the first part of the plan,
the jaquins distract Shuriki so
Elena and I can sneak into the palace.

Inside, we run into one of the castle servants.
He's just as happy to see Elena as everyone else is. So he
helps us find my family, and together, we free them!

Now it's time to save Elena's family!

We all rush to the Throne Room.

Mateo uses one of his grandfather's spells to free Elena's family from the painting.

"Isabel!" Elena cries, hugging her sister. "I missed you so much!"

I'm **so** happy for Elena!

But we still need to find Shuriki and take back the kingdom.

It's time for the final part of the plan.

The jaquins lead Shuriki outside . . .
to find me and Elena, our families, and
the entire city of Avalor ready to
face her—together!

"Leave **my palace** at once!" Shuriki commands.

"This was never **your** palace!" says Elena.

"You **can't stop** all of us!"

Shuriki smirks.
"I don't have to stop
everybody," she says.
"Just you."

She lifts her wand, but Chancellor Esteban
grabs it right out of Shuriki's hand!
"It's the source of her magic,"
he says, tossing it to Elena.

Elena snaps the wand in half.
"No!" Shuriki cries.

With her magic powers gone, she turns into an old woman and then runs away!

Avalor is **free** once more!
"All hail Princess Elena, the rightful
heir of Avalor!" shouts Chancellor Esteban.
"Princess Elena!" the people cheer.

"Thank you, Sofia," says Elena.

"I couldn't have done all this without a brave and clever friend like you."

As soon as we return to Enchancia, I hurry to the Secret Library and tell Alacazar what happened. "You helped give Elena's story an excellent ending," he says. "Actually," I tell him, "I have a feeling Elena's story is just beginning."

Introducing
Princess Elena of Avalor

·····················

Hola and hello!
My name is

ELENA

I am so **thankful** to Sofia for freeing me from
the amulet and helping me return home.
I love everything about **Avalor**—its beautiful
coastline, its snow-capped mountains, its rich history.
But most of all I **love** the people.

As the **Crown Princess of Avalor,** I am responsible for the entire kingdom. It takes patience, confidence, and a positive attitude to be a great leader. In a few years I'll be queen. But I have **a lot** to learn before that happens.

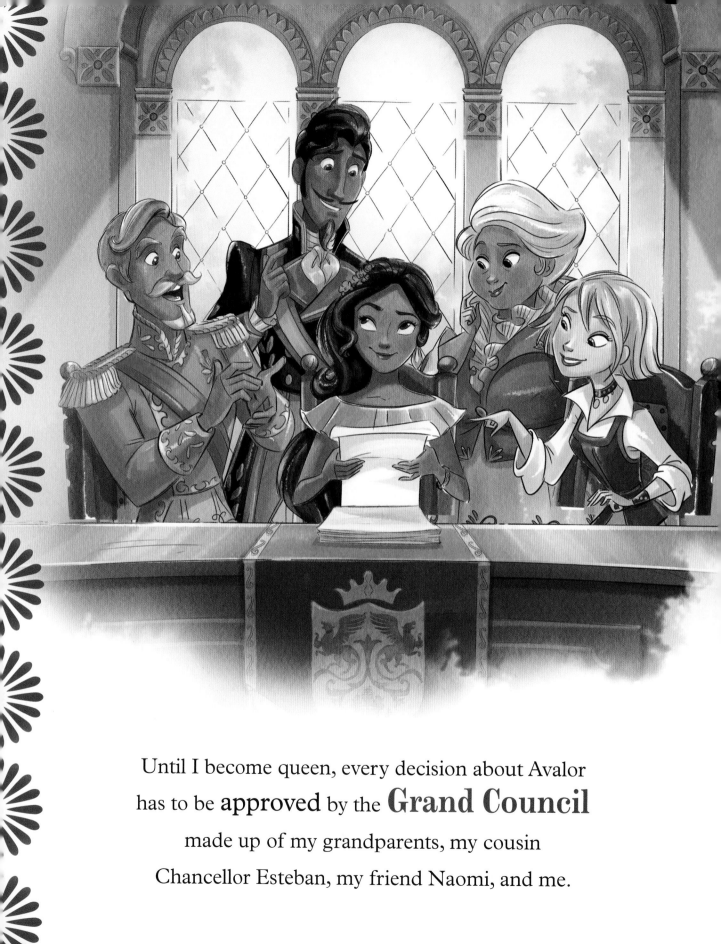

Until I become queen, every decision about Avalor
has to be **approved** by the **Grand Council**
made up of my grandparents, my cousin
Chancellor Esteban, my friend Naomi, and me.

On top of my royal duties, I take care of my little sister, **Isabel**. Isa is sweet and so smart. She's an **inventor**, and she can **fix almost** anything!

My *abuelito,* Francisco, has so many stories to tell. And Luisa, my *abuelita,* is **full** of **love** for our home and family. Together, we like to make **music** and sing.

I don't know what I would do without my **three best friends**.

I chose my friend **Mateo** to be **Avalor's Royal Wizard**, just like his grandfather was.

My friend **Gabe** is on the **Royal Guard** and is always looking out for me. Sometimes I think he worries too much, but I know I can count on him.

Naomi's family is in charge of the ships that arrive in Avalor City, so she knows people from all over. Her understanding of the world is really helpful on the **Grand Council**.

Avalor is **full** of **magical** creatures. You'd think meeting one would be scary, but it's actually really fun! Skylar, Migs, and Luna are **jaquins**—half jaguar and half bird!

I love it when they take me on exciting rides, soaring high above our kingdom. And **Zuzo** the Spirit Fox often gives me advice.

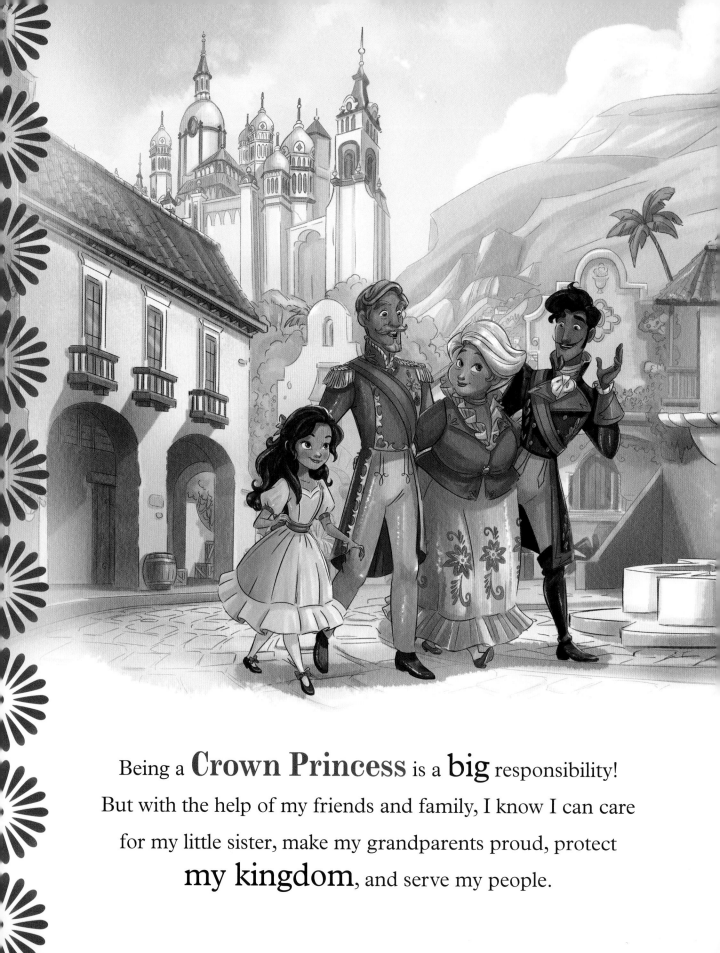

Being a **Crown Princess** is a **big** responsibility!
But with the help of my friends and family, I know I can care
for my little sister, make my grandparents proud, protect
my kingdom, and serve my people.

No one said **being** in **charge** would be easy,
but I am ready for the challenge. I can't wait till

᠅⁓ **I'm ready to rule!** ⁓᠅